D0020815

CELEBRATE THE TEMPORARY

CELEBRATE THE TEMPORARY

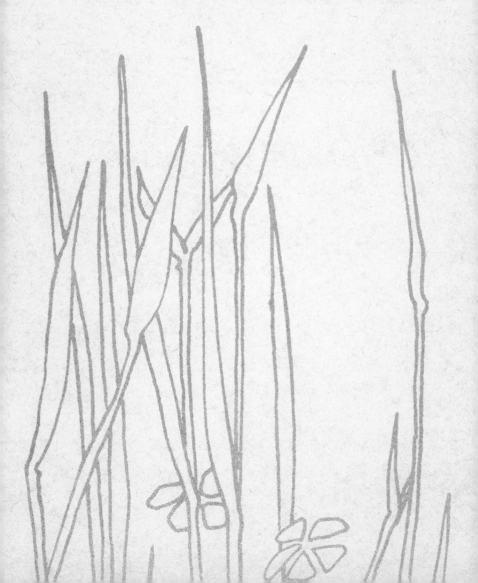

by Clyde Reid

Illustrations by Patricia Collins

HARPER & ROW, PUBLISHERS

New York
Hagerstown
San Francisco
London

Celebrate the Temporary. Copyright © 1972 by Clyde H. Reid.
All rights reserved. Printed in the United States of America. No
part of this book may be used or reproduced in any manner
whatsoever without written permission except in the case of brief
quotations embodied in critical articles and reviews. For
information address Harper & Row, Publishers, Inc., 10 East 53rd
Street, New York, N.Y. 10022. Published simultaneously in
Canada by Fitzhenry & Whiteside Limited, Toronto.

First Harper & Row paperback edition published 1974.

ISBN: 0-06-066817-2
ISBN: 0-06-066816-4 (paperback)

LIBRARY OF CONGRESS CATALOG CARD NUMBER: 73-160643

To Jennifer

Contents

Preface

Celebrate the Temporary is a personal book. It comes out of my own pilgrimage, my experiences of growth and insight from many directions, especially my encounters with the human potential movement.

In this book I invite you to live more fully in present experience, rather than focusing life in the future or the past. I talk about ways in which we can relax more into present (temporary) experience by really tasting our food, really feeling our pain, really seeing a single flower.

Modern man tends to race through life, not really tasting, smelling, seeing, feeling, or hearing. He has become so highly intellectualized that he has lost touch with his senses and feelings.

This book, drawing on experiences from the field of sensory awareness, yoga, and encounter, suggests some concrete, nonthreatening ways in which the

average person can "come to his senses." It invites
you to let go and live to some extent in the present
moment—without sacrificing concern for the future or
the reality of the past.

I invite you to embrace the cold and the snow as
friends instead of rejecting them as enemies or
opponents. I invite you to breathe into your pain and
celebrate that instead of sealing it off. I invite you to be
more aware of the gifts of breath and water and food by
calling your attention quite simply to the profundity
of these everyday, simple elements of life and
suggesting that you try some experiments with them.

If I were not so wrapped up in celebrating the
temporary myself, I would write a longer preface. Why
don't you read this and join me?

Clyde Reid

Denver, Colorado

9

Our swaddled and weary senses restrain us in a mysterious land of suspension and removal which has the qualities of distance and separation. We let nothing really touch us and become slaves to automatic living, paying very little notice to what goes on around us. Thus, we deny ourselves the fullness of living in the now, which requires that we must be able to open fully our senses and to direct our awareness.

Herbert A. Otto, "Sensory Awakening through Smell, Touch, and Taste," in *Ways of Growth,* ed. Herbert Otto and John Mann (New York: Grossman Publishers, 1968), p. 50.

*What is the use of planning to be able to eat next week
unless I can really enjoy the meals when they come? If
I am so busy planning how to eat next week that I
cannot fully enjoy what I am eating now, I will be in
the same predicament when next week's meals
become "now."*

*If my happiness at this moment consists largely in
reviewing happy memories and expectations, I am but
dimly aware of this present. I shall still be dimly aware
of the present when the good things that I have been
expecting come to pass. For I shall have formed a
habit of looking behind and ahead, making it difficult
for me to attend to the here and now. If, then, my
awareness of the past and future makes me less aware
of the present, I must begin to wonder whether I am
actually living in the real world.*

Alan W. Watts, *The Wisdom of Insecurity* (New York: Vintage Books,
1951), p. 35.

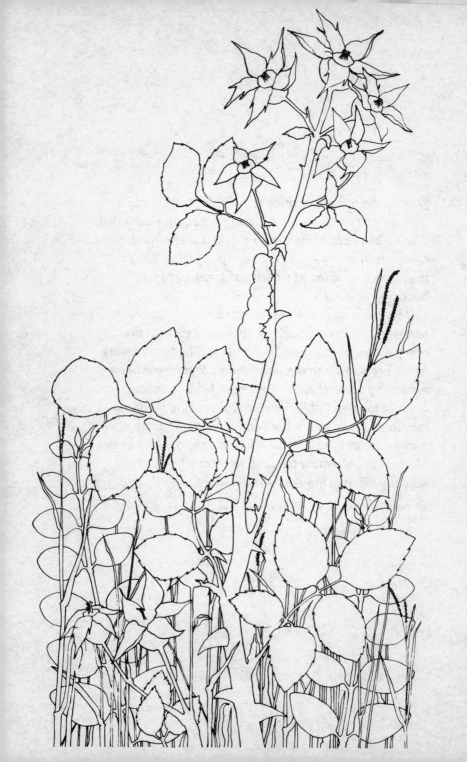

CELEBRATE THE TEMPORARY
DON'T WAIT UNTIL TOMORROW
LIVE TODAY

CELEBRATE THE SIMPLE THINGS
ENJOY THE BUTTERFLY
EMBRACE THE SNOW
RUN WITH THE OCEAN
DELIGHT IN THE TREES

OR A SINGLE LONELY FLOWER

GO BAREFOOT
IN THE WET GRASS

Don't wait
    until all the problems
    are solved
    or all the bills
    are paid

You will wait forever
Eternity will come and go
    and you
    will still be waiting

Live in the now
    with all its problems
    and its Agonies
    with its Joy
    and its Pain

CELEBRATE YOUR PAIN
YOUR DESPAIR
YOUR ANGER
IT MEANS YOU'RE ALIVE
LOOK CLOSER
BREATHE DEEPER
STAND TALLER
STOP GRIEVING THE PAST

THERE IS JOY AND BEAUTY
TODAY

IT IS TEMPORARY
HERE NOW AND GONE

SO CELEBRATE IT
WHILE YOU CAN
CELEBRATE THE TEMPORARY

Live in the Now

Celebrate the temporary. Live in the now.

I mean *right now,* not later this afternoon. Not after awhile. Not in a few hours, when the dishes are done and the kids are in bed. Not next week, when the in-laws have left. Not next year, when you're caught up on the doctor bills.

I mean celebrate now. Today. This minute. There is something in your life to celebrate right now! Sure, maybe you've had a tough life. Maybe you've just had some bad news. Maybe the company has been laying people off and you're out of a job and scraping by. Maybe you've had illness in your family and you have a mountain of bills. Okay.

Perhaps things have been going pretty smoothly, for that matter. Maybe you've had good news and the family's all well. Everything seems under control for the moment, but life still seems a bit flat. How come?

18

I want you to try something.

It won't take long. You can spare five minutes. Can't you?

First, remove whatever distractions you can. Turn off the radio or television set if it is playing. It will still be there when you come back. Or if you're lucky enough to have a quiet room, go there. Dim the lights or turn them off.

Now stand. Plant your feet squarely on the floor about six inches apart. Close your eyes. Put your shoulders back and stand straight. Take a deep breath and let some of the tension in you ride out with your breath. Permit yourself to relax inside.

Take another deep breath, inhaling gradually and feeling your breath slowly fill your abdomen and your chest. Do this several times, and concentrate on how it feels to stand relaxed and breathe into your own depth and your own strength.

WHAT A GIFT IS BREATH
THE SUPPLIER OF LIFE
AND STRENGTH

THANK GOD
FOR BREATH

Now that you've read this far, put the book down and try it; give yourself the gift of five minutes of breathing. When you've done that, come back and read a little further.

You see, you do have something to celebrate. Life. Breath. Life-giving breath. Celebrate the fact that you are alive and breathing. Feel the celebration in your stomach. Feel it in your chest.

TO CELEBRATE THE TEMPORARY
IS TO BREATHE DEEP INTO YOUR STRENGTH
TO PLAN FOR TOMORROW

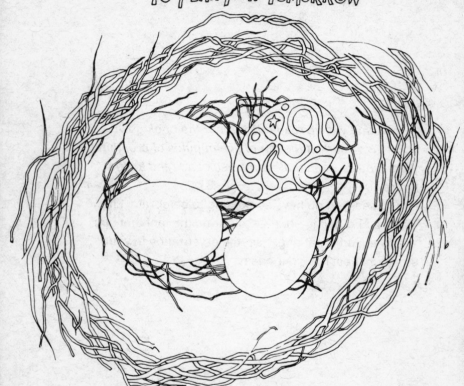

THEN LEAVE TOMORROW
TO TAKE CARE OF ITSELF
AND CELEBRATE BEING ALIVE TODAY

Many people do not know how to celebrate the temporary.

Some of my friends live constantly for tomorrow. They are always working and planning for that great future day when everything will be under control, when they can relax at last and begin to enjoy life. Sometimes even their bodies are bent forward, straining into the future.

And, of course, that great tomorrow never comes. It is always coming. Tomorrow. Their life style is a tomorrow style, and when tomorrow comes they do not know how to celebrate it because they did not learn how to live for today. So they must wait for another tomorrow—which never comes.

Maybe they do retire and move to Florida.

Maybe they do get that cabin in the woods.

Maybe they do buy their own home and get that second car.

There is always something more. Better neighbors or a new addition to the house or replacing the old car. They do not know how to relax into the present. To enjoy the now. To celebrate the temporary because that may be all we have.

I would not for a moment suggest that we forget the future. I do not believe in living only for today. I believe in planning ahead, preparing myself for the future, nourishing some dreams. To live only in the moment is a form of escapism. But that is not what I mean by celebrating the temporary. Nor is living only in the moment a danger for most of the people I know. Only once in a great while do I meet someone who lives for momentary pleasure alone.

The danger for most of us is living too much for the great future to come—or living in the past. That is the other danger, and it is just as sad to see.

We all know persons who live mainly on bygones, who spend most of their time and energy grieving over what has happened. Or what did not happen. Lamenting how it might have been, if only . . . They are "if only" people, living on their own grief and the sympathy of those who will suffer with them.

They do not know how to celebrate the temporary either. They are too busy enjoying the pain of the past. Their bodily posture is the bowed head and hunched shoulders.

Another way to live in the past is to keep recelebrating what happened in "the good old days." The athlete who must review the big game with his friends whenever they get together. Those who begin every conversation with "Remember the time when . . ." or "What is so-and-so doing now?"

Some reviewing of the past and of celebrative moments is good. When it becomes an exclusive style of life, it is boring and limits the celebrating of new experience.

I have visited old friends and spent an evening talking about past events and mutual acquaintances. When I have come away, I have often felt a sense of frustration at having lived only in the past. Something dies when relationships get stuck in this reviewing of past history with no new input of fresh experiencing. Some of each deepens a friendship.

I do not mean to look down on "if only" people nor on "just wait until tomorrow" people. Sometimes I am an "if only" person myself. Sometimes I'm a "tomorrow" person. There are times, inescapably, when all of us assume this stance. But the "if only" stance and the "tomorrow" stance can become frozen into a life style—if we do not learn as well how to celebrate the temporary, to live *also* for today.

I'm looking out the rain-blurred window of a big jet pulling out of LaGuardia on a foggy evening as darkness falls. An old impulse almost speaks, "If only the window were clear so I could see everything clearly!" Then I reject the old impulse. Go away. I do not need you.

To celebrate the now is to enjoy *the blurred colored lights on the landing strip seen through the fragmenting raindrops on my unclear window.*

TO ENJOY THEIR UNCLEARNESS
   THEIR BEAUTIFUL BLURRINESS
TO ENJOY WHAT IS
   AS IT IS
      FOR WHAT
         IT IS
            IN ITSELF

TO CELEBRATE THE NOW
   IS TO GO UP
      ON THE MOUNTAIN
   AND TAKE OFF
         YOUR GLASSES
            SOMETIMES

AND ENJOY THE LIGHTS
OF THE CITY DOWN BELOW
BLURRED AND LOVELY

In the pages that follow I will share with you some dimensions of celebrating the temporary. I invite you to think about this theme with me and at the same time do some exploring on your own.

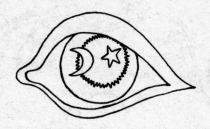

Taste, Feel, Touch, Listen, See

To celebrate the temporary is to taste, to feel, to touch, to appreciate with all the senses what is around you *right now.* "That's ridiculous," you may be thinking. "I do that all the time—so what's new?"

It's true, we taste, feel, touch, listen, and see all the time. But we do it *without awareness!* Our heads are so often in another place that we don't really taste what we are eating. We don't really enjoy what we are touching, don't realize the pleasure in the simple things we are doing.

I remember the occasion when I instructed members of a workshop to take ten minutes to walk outside in silence, letting something of beauty draw them. The workshop was being held on the grounds of a Benedictine monastery, surrounded by St. John's University in Minnesota. Several monks who lived on the campus were attending the workshop. I asked members of the group to relax, to breathe deeply, to let the beauty around them into their awareness.

A short while later the group began drifting back inside. I shall never forget one monk who said, "I've lived here most of my life. But this morning, in ten minutes, I saw things I have walked by for years and never noticed."

For most of us there is some beauty around us day by day. We sit beside it or look past it or ignore it. We fail to let it speak to our spirits, to call out to the beauty within us. We are somewhere else, living for tomorrow or fretting over the past.

I invite you to try a simple experiment for yourself. It will take only twenty or thirty minutes out of your life. Lie down on the floor, inhale and tense every muscle in your body as you hold your breath. Then exhale as you let the tension go and relax into the floor. Take another deep breath and let the tension in your body go out as you exhale. If you feel tightness somewhere, try to let it go.

When you feel relaxed, and if you have not fallen asleep, give yourself ten minutes to walk slowly, gracefully, and easily in your yard or a nearby park. The experience will have more power if you are sharing it with someone else. You should remain silent during the walk, however, and share observations afterward.

Try to be present to whatever beauty calls you. It may be the intricate patterns in a single flower blossom. It may be the winter sky. It may be an ordinary rock which calls you to it. Or it may be the variations of color and shadow in a single tree.

The main thing is not to try to program what happens. Don't decide your route in advance. *Just be.* Just flow with whatever your feelings lead you to. Just exist, with no plan, no program, no schedule. Is it too much to give yourself ten minutes just to be? *Why not try it now before you read further?*

Another helpful experience to heighten your awareness is to give your total attention to one flower or leaf or tree. Study it at close range, just permitting its beauty, its color, and its shape to speak to you. Then move a little closer to the subject and study it from that vantage point. Let it call out of you the sense of wonder and appreciation—the feeling of joy. Then move closer yet. Each time you do, you will see an entirely new world which you had not noticed before. When possible, share this with a partner afterward.

I shall long remember the night Carol brought the lilacs. I was a member for a time of a small house-church group, meeting weekly for conversational sharing and creative worship. Carol had agreed to provide leadership that week. It was lilac season, and she arrived with an armful—fresh, fragrant, lavender. She gave us each a large lilac cluster and asked us to study it in silence for awhile.

It was an experience of genuine pleasure just to be with those lilacs for a time. We held them, touched them, felt their texture, smelled them, touched them to our faces. One of the most pleasant parts of the evening was sharing memories and associations with lilacs. Each of us had some childhood experiences with

a lilac bush in the yard of our home or that of a neighbor.

Lilacs are a delight, and we tend to walk past them each spring without really stopping to see them, feel them, smell them, and appreciate them. We say, "Oh, isn't that nice. The lilacs are out again." When we next think about them, they are gone. Lilacs come and go very quickly, and to appreciate them fully we must celebrate the temporary, giving some of ourselves to the lilacs.

TO CELEBRATE THE TEMPORARY
IS TO LIE
ON YOUR BACK
ON THE FLOOR
IN THE DARK
AND LISTEN
REALLY
LISTEN
TO A BEAUTIFUL PIECE
OF MUSIC
NOT DOING
ANYTHING
ELSE
BUT

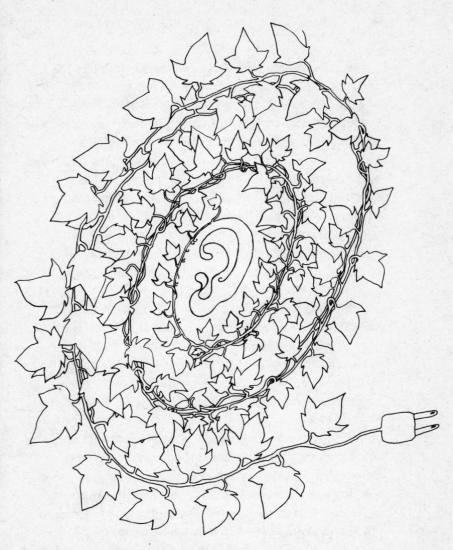

LISTENING
   WITH EVERY FIBER
      OF YOUR BEING

I was once leading a five-day workshop for clergy and wives in the Pacific Northwest. We were in a cabin on Puget Sound, and it had rained most of the week —which is usual in the Northwest. But about four o'clock in the afternoon of the fourth day, the clouds broke and the sun burst through. We were in the middle of our afternoon group session. Our response was spontaneous. We all rushed outside and stood in the sunshine, glorying in its warmth, its brilliance, in the glimpse of snow-covered mountain peaks which had been obscured all week. We laughed; we shouted; we danced around. We celebrated the temporary beauty and glory of the sun.

Fifteen minutes later the sun had disappeared again behind gray clouds. But I still remember with joy that brief dance in the sun and how delightful it was.

I had a similar experience once in Florida, where I was leading an intensive group workshop. We were gathering for our evening session, and a full moon was already well up in the sky. Fleecy clouds were racing across the sky, creating beautiful patterns of light and shadow as they obscured the moon, then revealed it. Rather than ignore this rare spectacle, we delayed our meeting and moved outside. We gathered on the shore of the lake and spent fifteen minutes just watching the moon and clouds in awe. It was a wonder-full way to begin the evening. We celebrated the temporary.

One of the crucial insights to grasp if you would celebrate the temporary is the importance of coming to your senses. Our culture has trained us so well to live in our intellect that we have literally lost touch with our senses. We simply do not hear the messages. We do not listen to the wisdom of our body, the guidance of our intuition. This is a grievous loss, and we need to get our senses and our intellect back into communication with each other. This is not to slight the importance of the intellect. On the contrary, the mind is enhanced when it is informed by the reality processes of the senses.

If you wish to work toward celebrating the temporary with your whole self, then three things are necessary. All three are incredibly simple. One is relaxing. The second is breathing. And the third is depriving yourself by turning off the sound of your voice in order to allow your senses to emerge.

Our bodies are amazing vehicles. They can carry tensions around inside them, locked into the muscles, for years and years. These tensions—the result of anger, fear, grief—can block us from perceiving the beauty around us, the support of the earth, the warmth and love of others. So it is essential to learn how to relax and release the tensions that block us from the full experience of life—with all our senses. I will say some more about relaxing in the section "On Letting Go."

Breathing is essential. I am convinced that most people do not breathe properly. Too many of us breathe shallowly, using only the upper portion of our lungs. This means we do not breathe into our potential, our depth, our strength. It also means that we inhibit the internal communication which breathing carries as it flows in and out. We lock our muscles in such a way as to prevent full breathing, and in so doing we prevent full living. We shut off the messages of our strength, our joy, our pain, our sexuality. We may feel "safer" that way, but the consequences in shallow living are a high price to pay.

Many disciplines today are teaching us the importance of deep breathing. Yoga begins with training in breathing, and I have learned much from my practice of yoga. The field of sensory awareness, as taught by Charlotte Selver and Charles Brooks, stresses breathing and relaxing into more creative functioning. Some newer forms of psychotherapy now stress breathing as a basic resource for health. Among these forms is Alexander Lowen's bio-energetic analysis.

When we relax and breathe more deeply, we are more in touch with our intuitive self, our feeling self, our instinctive wisdom, as well as our logical wisdom. We are more able to trust, to risk, to let life flow.

Members of a workshop I was leading at Iliff School of Theology decided to celebrate the temporary one beautiful summer evening. They had invited a number of persons from the community to join them and "celebrate a summer evening." Members of the workshop planned and led the experience, which was designed to help individuals who did not know each other discover an experience of community in only a few hours.

When everyone had gathered, we stood in a circle, took a few deep breaths and let go some of the tension in our bodies. Each of us then found a partner and sat silently to watch a magnificent Colorado sunset over the Rockies. The unbelievable colors in the clouds, the quiet and cool of the evening, all combined to make the occasion one of depth and meaning.

Yet we do not need spectacular sunsets to celebrate the temporary. We can celebrate the temporary in the delicious smell of coffee perking in the morning. The feeling of cold water running over our hands and faces. The smell of lime shaving cream. The taste of fresh oranges. The smell of a rose. The touch of a child's hand.

To celebrate the Temporary
    is to wade
        in a stream
        BAREFOOT
        And
            REALLY
            Feel
        THE COLD WATER
        RUNNING THROUGH YOUR TOES

To WALK IN THE WARM SAND
        AND LISTEN To THE OCEAN

To CLIMB A TREE
        AND LOOK DOWN
            AT THE WORLD BELOW

To WATCH A BIRD

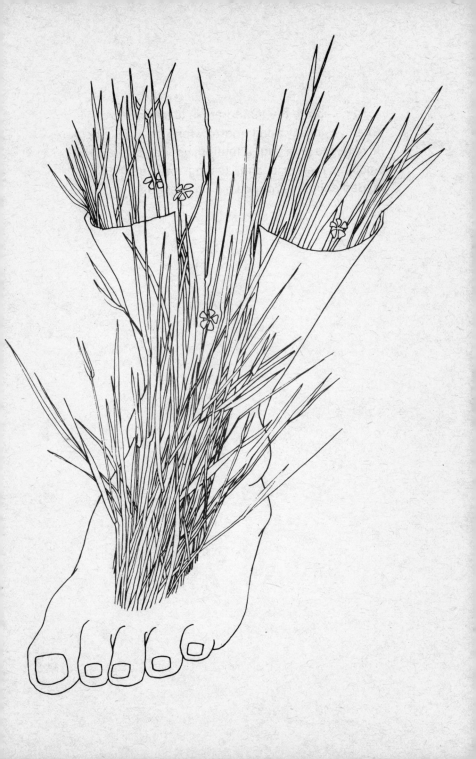

To celebrate the temporary is to let go of worrying about yesterday and tomorrow long enough to be *here, now*. It is to give your attention, your awareness, to smelling, feeling, seeing, tasting, and hearing the myriad delights around you. To live today.

Lean into Your Pain

One of the most common obstacles to celebrating the temporary is our avoidance of pain. We dread pain. We fear pain. We do anything to escape pain. Our culture reinforces our avoidance of pain by assuring us that we can live a painless life.

Advertisements constantly encourage us to believe that life can be pain-free. There is a remedy and an easy escape from every hurt—novocain from the dentist, anesthesia before the stitches, pain-killers for the headache. Alcohol or drugs to kill the pain of an awkward social situation or personal crisis.

To live without pain is a myth. It is possible to live *virtually* without pain by cutting yourself off from your feelings. The pain is in you, but the message does not reach your consciousness. Many people live this way, like walking zombies, rather than allow themselves to feel pain.

To live without pain, however, is to live half-alive, without fullness of life. This is the unmistakable, clear, unalterable fact. The more we escape pain, the more it comes back to haunt us in other ways. When it comes, we are unprepared for it and there is no escape.

I am not proposing that we go about looking for painful experiences—like putting our hand on a hot stove to prove we are alive. If the pain of having a tooth repaired is too intense, then surely we should have it deadened. But should we demand novocain every time, before we even know how much it will hurt? Should we not be able to live with some pain? The danger is living deadened lives, avoiding the experience of pain at any cost.

We sometimes stuff our mouths beyond our need for nourishment in order to deaden our feelings. By keeping our attention in our mouths, we can ignore the anxiety signals coming from our insides.

But there is another way to live. A more satisfying way. To help you feel into this other way, I'd like to invite you to try a simple experiment. There is a basic yoga position which helps to dramatize the experience of leaning into pain. You sit on the floor with both legs extended before you. You should be wearing loose clothing, no shoes.

You take the right foot and place it inside your left thigh as high up the leg as it will reach. Then extend both arms high above the head with your thumbs locked together. Slowly bring the arms forward, reaching for the left foot and bringing the head down toward the left knee. Unless you are unusually loose, you will probably reach a point where it hurts as you come down.

When you hit that point of pain, concentrate on the precise point of the pain. Say to yourself, "That's where it hurts—right there." You may find that you have a tendency to pull back from the pain when you hit it. That is a life style for many people—retreating from the first hint of pain. But try this time to lean into the pain, look it in the eye and see what happens. *Why not stop reading now and try it. When you hit the point of pain, concentrate on it and relax into it. Take a deep breath and lean a little lower. It will only take a few minutes to try this, and the rest of the chapter will make more sense to you if you do.*

The fascinating discovery of most people trying the simple head-knee pose is that pain is not all that bad. By concentrating attention on the pain, and by relaxing into it, the pain tends to diminish *or disappear.* Leaning into life's pain can also be a life style, and is far more satisfying than the avoidance style. It requires small doses of plain courage to look pain in the eye, but it prepares you for more serious pain when it comes. In the meantime, all the energy expended to avoid pain is now available for the business of living.

What many of us do not realize is that pain and joy run together. When we cut ourselves off from our pain, we have unwittingly cut ourselves off from joy as well. To allow yourself to feel pain is to allow yourself to feel. To prevent pain, you also prevent other feelings because you have blocked off the messages from your body. You may *think* you experience joy, but the experience of joy encompasses the whole body, not just the head.

45

TO CELEBRATE THE TEMPORARY
IS TO LIE IN BED
A FEW MINUTES
WHEN YOU FIRST WAKE UP
WATCHING
THE SUN
COMING THROUGH
THE WINDOW
THE REFLECTIONS
ON THE CEILING
THE COLORS
IN THE ROOM
AND
THANKING
GOD
FOR
LIFE

I was leading a workshop one day for Roman Catholic priests and nuns who work as campus pastors around the country. At one point the group was divided into units of five or six, sitting at round tables for discussion. As I slid my chair up to listen to one group, a young woman was talking about her feeling of emptiness after an enjoyable weekend. Tears filled her eyes and she put her head down and cried.

As she talked about her emptiness, she mentioned her hesitation to form deep attachments with anyone at the workshop. She didn't want the pain of giving up another friend. She told us how she had experienced a great sense of loss as every close friend in her life had died or left her within a brief span of time. "I have no one left."

It had hurt so much to give up her friends that she couldn't imagine giving up anyone else—even a temporary friend. She could not celebrate temporary relationships because she feared the pain of losing them. And so she continued as a lonely, empty person, unable to experience deep joy or deep pain.

That may have been all she could do at that time. I suspect most of us have gone through similar periods in our lives. There are times when our losses seem to accumulate and we feel we must withdraw for awhile into our psychological shells and lick our wounds, protecting ourselves from further pain until our strength returns.

Others seem to live constantly by the same numbing principle which the young woman was experiencing— even when their losses are not so grievous. They withdraw into emptiness at the approach of pain, living empty lives in their unwillingness to risk the possibility of further pain. Or any pain at all.

To celebrate the temporary
is to really take time
to taste bread
To give it
your full attention
For just a few minutes
to smell it
Touch it
To chew it slowly
While it dissolves
in your mouth
To think about bread
And the life it brings
The strength it gives

I encountered an interesting example of the avoidance style when I spent a year in Topeka, Kansas. I was a Research Fellow at the Menninger Foundation, one of the nation's leading centers for the study of psychiatry. I soon became aware of the fact that there was a community of "permanent people" in Topeka and a number of smaller groups of "temporary" people. The permanent people were the Topeka residents who more or less had their roots in that community. The temporary people were those who had come to study at the Foundation and knew they would be in the city for only a year or possibly three years.

The permanent people tended to avoid deep contacts with temporary people, their friends usually being other permanent residents. On rare occasions a permanent resident would become involved in the life of a temporary person and allow a friendship to blossom. Since this seemed to be the exception, however, the temporary people sought each other out for their friendships. Deeper and closer relationships developed because of their temporary nature.

I decided that the permanent people avoided us temporary types because they did not want the pain of giving us up. If they allowed themselves to like us, it meant they would miss us when we left. So it was easier to avoid involvement and thereby avoid the pain of letting us go! By avoiding the pain of involvement, they also cheated themselves and us of potential joy.

The interesting thing is that all our relationships are temporary. Can you think of a single permanent relationship? Mother? Father? An old and dear friend? They all die eventually. Or move away. Or change. Just as you and I change and grow. If we cushion ourselves against deep involvement because someday we may lose the person, we only cheat ourselves and them as well.

So why not celebrate those relationships now while we have them? And while we can appreciate them? Even if we have them for just a day, or a week, or a year.

I was sitting with an old friend on the campus at Berkeley one warm spring Sunday afternoon. The sidewalks and courtyards were swarming with people out for a stroll in the sun. Pete and I sat on the cement for a time, listening to an informal group of musicians beating out primitive rhythms on an assortment of bongo drums and old cowbells.

It was fascinating to watch the faces in the crowd around that pulsating musical heart. People just enjoying each other, enjoying their right to be free, to wear odd clothes or go barefoot. There were children hanging from the branches of the tree under which the musicians beat out their ancient music.

We were reminiscing that day, Pete and I. Recalling the day we had played hookey from high school classes for a walk in the park and had to face the dean . . . Remembering old girlfriends . . . And double dating

. . . And we talked about my kid brother, Jim.

Jim was killed in an Air Force jet crash in Portland, Oregon. Jim and his pilot were patrolling the Northwest coast during the Korean War. Jim was flying radar observer. The jet simply went dead in the air one day. He and his pilot could have bailed out, but they rode the plane into a clump of trees to avoid hitting the homes nearby where children were playing. (I remember sitting through Jim's funeral without crying. I thought I was being strong then, but now I know I just wasn't allowing myself to feel the pain that was there. I had to do my crying for Jim years later—and may still have some to do.)

I was the brother who made the headlines, but Jim was the one everybody loved. Who was the more successful? Is success measured in becoming known, or is it in loving and being loved?

Pete and I grieved awhile that day about the loss of a young man we had both cared about deeply. Our conversation went something like this:

Pete: What a tragic thing it is when life can be snuffed out like that! What a loss. He's gone and there's nothing we can do about it.

Me: That's right, we can't do anything about it. But there is another way we can look at it.

Pete: What's that?

Me: Look, we both feel pain at losing Jim, because

we loved him. I don't want to deny that pain for a moment. But we can also rejoice that we had him for twenty-four years. We did know him, and he did enrich our lives during that time.

Why not celebrate what we did have rather than grieve what we can't have?

Pete: I really hadn't thought of it that way.

It often does not occur to us to celebrate the good, the joy, and the love that we have received. We spend our time feeling bad that we don't still have it today, and so today is dampened by that sadness and is not celebrated for itself.

We can make choices about our life style. We do every day. We can choose to live a life of regretting, an "if only" style. Or we can choose a realistic, sometimes regretting but basically celebrating style that focuses on the good *along with* the painful. That is celebrating the temporary.

When you have nothing else to celebrate, *celebrate your pain!* At least it proves you are alive.

On Letting Go

A young man once registered for a conference I was conducting on small group leadership. For the first few days he was uncommonly quiet and withdrawn. I had known him from a previous conference, and he had been much more alive and involved.

Finally I asked him, "Harvey, I notice that you have been distant and uninvolved since this conference began. Would you like to tell us why?"

"I guess I'm disappointed," he replied. "I attended a workshop here once before, and I was in a tremendous group. We really had a great time together. I guess I came here expecting to find that old group, and it's not like that at all." It became increasingly apparent that Harvey had not given up his old group when it ended, hoping to find it again. We talked for awhile about the necessity of giving up those things in life which hold us back from participating in the present.

Then we did an interesting thing. I handed Harvey an

imaginary shovel so he could "bury" his old group. He entered into the role play with great vigor, digging a grave in the middle of the floor. When he had finished, he shoved his "old group" into the imaginary hole. Others in the group joined in, shoving into the hole some things in their lives which they had been holding onto unnecessarily.

The "grave" was then filled up, and the group celebrated a new feeling of freedom for having given up some unneeded baggage. Nonverbal acting out is often more than symbolic. Some genuine changes can begin when the whole self is involved in such experiences, because we are dealing with *real feelings.* Harvey, for example, became an actively participating member of the conference from that moment. The change in his *behavior* was dramatic.

"Letting go" is an important dimension of creative living. It is difficult indeed to celebrate the temporary, to live fully in the present, when we are holding onto old emotional baggage which belongs to the past. Letting go has many aspects.

One of these aspects is the giving up of our need to control situations and persons. There are many people who are not comfortable unless they are in charge. They must control what happens and when it will happen. They fret under any leadership but their own. The result is that there are no surprises. And no joy. And no one grows but the leader.

I once worked with a group which exhibited a high degree of control. Its members had difficulty letting go and enjoying the freedom in whatever happened. For one evening session with that group, I proposed a "moonwalk."

The moonwalk is experienced in a large plastic tent with a plastic floor that bounces up and down and throws you around whenever anyone steps on it. To experience the moonwalk, you take off your shoes and crawl into the tent. You must be willing to give up control of much of your movement and permit yourself to be bounced around in a crazy fashion for about ten minutes. It can be excellent practice for letting go in order to celebrate the temporary.

It is important to recognize the direct relationship between letting go physically and psychologically. We are increasingly admitting the connection between the body and the emotions. Our very muscles "hold on" to old burdens, and if we can let go in the muscles, we can sometimes move past old hang-ups.

I would like to suggest a simple experiment in letting go for you to try. If you have a strong bar from which you can hang by your arms, or a swing set in the backyard or nearby playground, use that. Hang your full weight from the bar, holding on as tightly as you can. Feel how much energy it takes to hold on. Then relax and let go. Concentrate your attention on the sensation of letting go and see how good it feels.

I was at a picnic recently with some friends, and several of the children were playing on a swing set nearby. One three year old discovered a neat way to draw her parents' attention. She would stand up in her swing and grab hold of a bar about five feet off the ground. Then she would scream for help because she was "afraid" to let go. Time after time the mother or father would rush over to rescue her so she wouldn't have to risk letting go. She would have fallen about one foot to the ground. I hope that little girl learns to let go and take the consequences.

If you do not have a bar from which you can hang, lie on the floor and take a strong grip on a table leg or a convenient piece of furniture. Note how much strength it takes to hold on tightly. Then relax every muscle in your body and let go. You can practice letting go of things physically and see if there is any carry-over in your ability to let go in other ways. People who are constipated, verbally or otherwise, need practice in letting go.

Another aspect of letting go is to release the tensions within us and allow ourselves to *feel*. Many persons have not given themselves permission to have feelings, thereby blocking feelings from their awareness.

It may be that their parents did not give them permission to feel, frowning on expressions of feeling in the family and making it a virtual taboo. Many adults are walking around still carrying unwanted childhood taboos in their bodies. They have not given themselves permission to be adult and make their own decisions. And no one else can do it for them.

The need to know in advance exactly what will happen is another expression of control and holding on. So we find people gathering for worship with every detail planned in advance and printed in a program— to hear a sermon on the importance of allowing the Holy Spirit to guide their lives! When the element of surprise is gone, boredom sets in. When we can let go some of our compulsive controlling of the future, spontaneous and exciting things can begin to emerge.

The difficult truth to grasp is that when we do not let go, we often choke to death the beautiful things we had hoped to keep alive. When we do not let go of our children, our holding on too long kills something in them for us. "It's for their own good!" we say. "They're not ready to be turned loose!" Often it is our own need to hang on which prompts our behavior long after the children have been crying for us to let go.

The opposite is sometimes true as well. Children may have difficulty letting go of their parents, thus prolonging unduly their period of dependence.

I remember an occasion when members of a group I was leading were asked to walk outside on a winter day and to allow themselves to be drawn to something of beauty. One man came back inside, clutching a small handful of snow. The snow had so attracted him with its beauty that he could not let it go. He sat with that ball of snow in his hand, unable to leave it behind, and watched it turn to a lump of ice, then melt. Had he been able to let it go, it could have continued its life as snow.

Letting go means to be more free. Letting things happen. Letting life bring you surprises and challenges and joy. To let go some of the controls that bind us in is to let life flow instead of limiting life by channeling it all in advance. Like the friend who called up recently and said, "Some of us are going to the grocery store to get some things for a picnic. We'll be ready to eat in about an hour. Could you join us?" What is more delightful than a surprise picnic? Or more disappointing than one which is planned a month in advance and is rained out?

TO CELEBRATE THE TEMPORARY
IS TO GET RID
OF THAT HAIRDO
THAT PREVENTS
CELEBRATING
THAT CAN'T BE RAINED ON
OR TOUCHED
OR VIOLATED
BY ROLLING
DOWN A HILL

TO BE FREE OF ALL
THAT SELF-INFLICTED
BONDAGE
IS
TO CELEBRATE
THE TEMPORARY

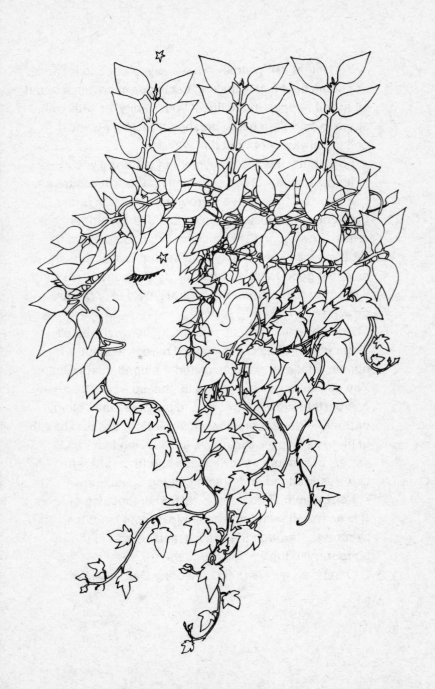

You might ask yourself what it is *you* need to let go. For some of you, it is making decisions in advance about what will happen in the life of your family, or with your spouse—and then being crushed and angry when it doesn't always work out that way.

For others, it is the enjoyment of suffering you need to let go. I have worked with many people in groups who complain that they have a problem. But when offered the opportunity to solve the problem, they suddenly realize how much they enjoy having it. Displaying their problem may keep them in the center. Even the pain may feel good to them. After all, their emotions reason, it is better to hurt than to be ignored. So they do not grow.

An interesting aspect of letting go is what we call "letting your child out to play." There is a beautiful human relations exercise called the blind trust walk. You ask members of a group to choose a partner, then one partner closes his eyes and becomes the "blind partner." The other leads him around for a stated length of time, perhaps ten minutes, introducing him to a variety of sensory experiences—touching different textures, walking and running, going up and down stairs, bumping into people, tasting or smelling objects. It is an excellent exercise to help people heighten awareness through the senses, and celebrate the temporary in the world around them.

One time I was leading an elderly Canadian lady as

my partner. At first she was very stiff and reserved. She did not want to touch objects I would hand her, reacting as though they might dirty her hands. As the walk proceeded, however, she began to loosen up and enjoy herself.

Then it was my turn to be the blind partner. As she began leading me, she relaxed further and began to enjoy the experience more and more. I suddenly had the sensation that there were two distinct people leading me—the elderly lady still held my wrist, but there was a little girl nearby, giggling and delighting in her freedom. My partner had "let her little girl out to play," and I could sense the difference dramatically. It was beautiful to feel—until her little girl ran me into a table at full speed!

It is a nice thing to let your child out to play once in awhile. Our adult roles call for us to be serious and "straight" so much of the time that we often forget to enjoy life. Yet Jesus calls us to "be as little children." It is delightful to experience people enjoying their "childness" occasionally.

I once went hiking in the Rockies with the Colorado Mountain Club. A friend and I hiked about three miles up a mountain slope to the top of a beautiful pass. The trail was covered from time to time by banks of snow which we had to cross. My friend and I would throw snowballs, or put ice down each other's backs. At one point we slid on a snowbank on the seat of our pants about fifty feet down the mountain slope. Within the bounds of reason and safety, we had "let our child out to play." It made the day even more exhilarating.

Possessing *people* is another thing some of us need to let go. I remember hearing a lady at a party ask a man, "Does she belong to you?" She indicated one of the women in the group. "No," he replied. "She is my wife, but she belongs to herself." Many people have the conviction that when you are married, you *belong* to your spouse.

The husband who feels that his wife is his property becomes quite upset if she has any deep friendships outside the marriage. In extreme cases, he will not even permit her to enjoy *talking* to another man, much less have a life of her own.

The same is true of the wife who feels she owns her husband. Such possessiveness kills relationships. It smothers love and builds frustration and boredom. It is one of the things we must learn to let go.

A corollary of this attitude of possessiveness is the feeling that we cannot have a relationship with someone unless it is a permanent, lifelong commitment. The person who believes this then restricts himself or herself to family and a few friends, ruling out temporary relationships. But temporary relationships, as we have seen, can have their own special beauty. They do not need to be permanent or total to have meaning.

I remember a young college student I once sat with

on an airplane trip. The flight was about thirty minutes long. But we got into a conversation that had both depth and meaning. We felt a special bond in the common understandings that emerged. A thirty-minute friendship may not seem like much, but it can be a thing of rare beauty. It has been years, and I have not forgotten it.

When we can give up the myth of permanence as a condition for sharing ourselves, we can celebrate temporary relationships as well as longer ones. After all, what is time? One day is a long time. One week is forever. One year is perhaps a seventieth of our whole life.

Sometimes people find a meaningful temporary friendship, then try to hang onto it. They quickly jot down names and addresses and promise to "look you up" at a later time. They have not learned to celebrate a relationship for its temporariness and let it go. They are caught in the mindset which says that a relationship to have meaning must be ongoing. Disappointment is often the result when we try to re-create a contact that had meaning in a particular place and time.

Letting go is a basic lesson of life, and is a necessity if we are to learn how to celebrate the temporary. We must let go of our bondage to possessions. We must let go of our family, our friends, even our life. So long as we cling to life as a permanent possession, it will not be as full as it can be. To be willing and ready to give it up at the right time is to celebrate the temporariness of life.

To die gracefully is to live fully. To cling too tightly to life is to kill it prematurely.

I find Jesus to be a man who knew how to celebrate the temporary. He taught us not to be anxious about tomorrow, but to let tomorrow take care of itself. And he knew how to enjoy a good party!

What do you need to let go? Why not make a short list of those things in your life you need to give up. Then decide which is most important and go to work on letting it go so you can more easily celebrate the temporary.

Embrace the Alien

We arrived at Chico Hot Springs on a Friday evening late in April. I was to lead a retreat on awareness for about seventy-five people from all over Montana. The site was an old hot springs resort tucked away in a valley of the Rockies not far from Yellowstone National Park. An outdoor mineral pool was fed by hot spring water gushing out of the mountainside. The ground was bare, as the winter's snow had vanished.

It started to rain as we began our evening session. By ten that night, the rain had changed to snow. Some of the braver spirits jumped into swimsuits and plunged out into the chill night air long enough to make it to the warm, soothing waters of the pool. The rising steam and swirling snow combined to create a misty fairyland. The icy snowflakes stung the face and body, while the water warmed you from beneath. We came out feeling alive and refreshed.

By morning an inch of fresh new snow covered the

ground, the tree limbs, and the fences. As our morning session began, I announced that we would put on our boots and coats and go silently out into the snow. A murmur ran through the group, as well as some audible groans. "Our temptation is to regard the snow as enemy," I said. "We so often encounter it as an obstacle, something to fight against on the highway, something to be shoveled out of the way. This morning I want you to try to embrace the snow as a friend. I want you to go out in silence, alone, and experience the snow for fifteen minutes. Walk in it, touch it, taste it, feel its texture, its temperature. Listen to its crunch underfoot. Relax and enjoy the snow as a gift. Let its beauty into your spirit. Then come back in and find a partner to share your experience with." (Imagine inviting Montanans to experience *snow!*)

The groans changed into the shuffle of boots being reluctantly pulled on, and the exodus was underway. It was an incredibly beautiful morning. The air was clear and crisp. The sky was bright blue with a few puffy clouds for accent. The snow was—well, it was just virgin snow.

We scattered around, walking, breathing, touching, throwing snowballs now and then, licking snow off fence posts. Listening to the morning sounds around us. Just groking on snow and beauty. On mountain slopes and evergreens dusted with white. It was delightful. Exhilarating. And refreshing to the spirit. We were experiencing awareness, not just talking about it. We were getting into the body and out of the head.

We were celebrating the temporary by embracing the alien—or something we too often regard as alien, as enemy. Winter's cold is also regarded that way. And yet when we breathe in the cold air deeply, it is refreshing and warming. When we huddle against the cold and try to shut it away from ourselves, then it does feel alien. When we breathe into the pain of the cold, we are more alive and awake and it does not seem nearly so alien.

Cold rain is often regarded as alien, too. I was having supper not long ago with my friends, Jim and Izzie. We had some great potato soup, with cheese and thick wheat bread. We were sitting on the living-room floor, talking and listening to rock music, when Izzie said, "Is that rain I hear?"

We jumped up and looked outside. It was pouring. A virtual cloudburst. Izzie said, "Let's run out in the rain!" So we shucked off our shoes and socks and darted out. We romped barefoot in the wet grass, whirling around and dancing in glee with the cold spring rain running down our faces and soaking our clothes. We celebrated the temporary by embracing the rain.

The opposite instinct is to protect ourselves from the

rain and from the possibility of getting wet. People most commonly huddle inside and close the windows when the rain begins.

"I don't want to catch my death of cold."

"My clothes will get all wet."

"People will think we're nuts if we do that."

But the experience of running in the rain was delicious. I had to take off my shirt and wear an old sweater of Jim's to get home, but who cares?

Embracing the alien includes alien people. I was teaching a course on personal growth at Iliff School of Theology when riots broke out in nearby Boulder, location of the University of Colorado. After a series of clashes with local police, the transient "street people" living in Boulder had lashed out in anger one night, breaking thousands of dollars' worth of store windows.

The riots raged on Friday and Saturday nights, and continued on Sunday night as well. On Monday morning my class jumped into cars and drove to Boulder. We paired off and spread out through the community, talking to and listening to street people, policemen, students, and businessmen. My partner and I were sipping coffee in a Boulder restaurant. In one of the booths we noticed two young men with leather vests, lengthy beards, bare tattooed arms, and long, unkempt hair. After sizing them up for awhile, my partner walked over to their table and asked if we could sit and talk with them. I followed her.

She embraced the alien by reaching out to relate to persons who were obviously members of a subculture we usually avoid. To our delight, they welcomed us to their booth, and for the next hour talked eagerly and earnestly about their experiences during the riots and their feelings as street people. We were given a greater awareness of the underlying causes of the Boulder riots and the concerns of persons in a minority group often mistreated and misunderstood. While we did not believe everything they told us, we did come away with deeper understanding.

Because we were able to risk rejection, we found acceptance and insight. The alien for you may be blacks, or Catholics, or theologians, or youths with long hair. Or little children. You will find yourself celebrating the temporary when you can risk reaching out to meet and know other kinds of people.
When you withdraw from people because they wear beards or have some characteristic that puts you off, you narrow your world and limit your possibilities.

TO CELEBRATE THE TEMPORARY
IS TO CARRY A CHILD
ON YOUR SHOULDERS
INSTEAD
OF WALKING
SEDATELY TO THE CAR

TO ROLL WITH THEM
IN THE GRASS

AND TOSS THEM
IN THE AIR

TO CELEBRATE CHILDREN

WHO ARE
THEMSELVES
TEMPORARY

I have often begun a workshop or conference by asking people to take off their shoes and socks. This idea is startling to many people, because they protect themselves from the sensations the feet can bring by wearing tight shoes and binding off those feelings. "My feet are too tender!" they say. "My feet hurt when I take my shoes off!" Of course they hurt when they are always protected from sensation. I will then ask the workshop participants to form a long line, holding hands. We will walk silently with bared feet across lawns, driveways, gravel paths, and whatever else the environment offers.

The responses are usually ones of delight. "I had forgotten how delightful it is to walk barefoot through the grass." "I felt more a part of nature than I have in years." My feet feel more alive than they have in a long time." "They still tingle." "I felt a kinship with the poor of the world who have no shoes." These are actual comments I have heard after such an experience. We tend to regard the grass and gravel and dirt as enemies to be avoided. In so doing, we cut ourselves off from many sensations of delight and deny our natural relationship to the earth.

It is possible to walk across grass or gravel with the feet tense, the muscles rigid, rejecting the sensations in the soles. Then the gravel *will be* an enemy, for its pressure against the rigid muscles will hurt. But if we walk relaxed, with the muscles of the feet at ease and accepting what comes, then the gravel will not hurt, or the occasional stone will not seem so large. We celebrate the temporary by relaxing into a relationship with whatever comes. When we embrace the alien—or what appears to be alien—we often discover it as friend.

Why not try this same experiment for yourself? Invite a friend or a member of your family to experience it with you. Take off your shoes and socks and take a barefoot walk in the yard or a nearby park. Feel the sidewalk, the grass, dig your toes into the dirt and enjoy it. Do it at least partly in silence. Allow your feet to feel.

When you have finished, take a large pan of warm water and soap and wash each other's feet in silence, enjoying the pleasant sensations of having your feet cared for. Give yourself permission to enjoy having your feet washed and relax into it.

Massage your partner's foot as you wash it, working into each muscle and each toe. Then rub some oil on the foot when it has been dried, and leave your warm hands for a moment on top of the foot. Share with your partner afterward some of the sensations and thoughts you experienced on the walk.

This is a beautiful experience to share with someone you love. It will help open communication with your senses—which God gave you to use and enjoy. Why not try it now? Put this book down and go.

One summer I attended an advanced workshop on

sensory awareness held on Monhegan Island in the Atlantic Ocean, ten miles off the coast of Maine. We had classes in the mornings and some evenings, but our afternoons were free for walking in the lovely primitive forest or climbing on the rugged cliffs. Sometimes we swam in the chill ocean, embracing the alien cold of the North Atlantic and finding refreshment and vigor. (Almost more vigor than I care to find. When I swam in those waters, it *was temporary!*)

We gathered one afternoon for a silent walk to experience the ocean shore. As we walked toward the cove which was our destination, we took off our shoes or sandals and put them in a pile, proceeding the rest of the way barefoot. The rugged little forest path looked alien indeed.

By relaxing into the walking, however, we found no difficulty. Once at the cove, we scattered around, listening to the crashing ocean, exploring some old shipwreck ruins, picking up rocks, investigating tidal pools, and climbing rocks. For many people the ocean is alien—a thing to be feared and avoided. Walking barefoot on the rocks is alien. Being quiet is alien. All of these became friends that afternoon.

I shall never forget an encounter I once had on a Greyhound bus riding into Detroit. I sat down next to a little old lady with gray hair and old-fashioned clothes.

My first impulse was something like this: "Well, this little lady and I surely have nothing in common. I hope she isn't talkative. I'm tired and I'd like to be left alone so I can read."

What a mistake it would have been if I had failed to get acquainted with that woman. We allowed each other our privacy for a time, but later we exchanged a few words. As the trip proceeded, we talked some more, and I discovered that she was an amazing personality. *She had been one of the first women pilots in the whole history of the world!* She was in her seventies at that time, and still maintained an active pilot's license.

In her youth she had flown barnstorming tours around the United States, flying old biplanes with some of the famous names in aviation. She was gathering memorabilia for an aviation museum from some of the original pilots still living. She was a delightful person, and we shared much about our personal pilgrimages and our interest in the spiritual life.

In her appearance she had at first seemed alien to me. By allowing myself to open up to her (as she did to me), I discovered a temporary friendship I could enjoy, celebrate, and treasure. I still celebrate that brief encounter. You never know what rare personality may be seated next to you—nor does the person need to be famous to be worth knowing.

OPEN YOURSELF
TO THE POSSIBILITIES
             AROUND YOU
GO BAREFOOT
    IN THE COOL GRASS

RUN OUT
    INTO THE SNOW
    AND RUB IT
        IN YOUR HAIR
    YOU'LL DRY OUT

EMBRACE THE ALIEN

RISK A RELATIONSHIP
WITH SOMEONE
        STRANGE TO YOU

LIVE IN THE NOW
CELEBRATE THE TEMPORARY

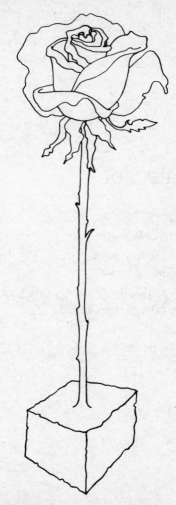

CELEBRATE LIFE

Celebrate You

Celebrate you!
You are worth celebrating.
You are worth everything.
You are unique.
In the whole world, there is only one you.
There is only one person with
  your talents
  your experiences
  your gifts.

NO
ONE
CAN TAKE
YOUR
PLACE

God created only one you, precious in his sight.
You have immense potential
   to love
   to care
   to create
   to grow
   to sacrifice
   if you believe in yourself.
It doesn't matter your age, or your color, or whether
   your parents loved you or not. (Maybe they wanted
   to but couldn't.) Let that go. It belongs to the past.
   You belong to the now.
It doesn't matter what you have been. The wrong you've

done. The mistakes you've made. The people you've
  hurt.
You are forgiven. You are accepted. You're okay. You
  are loved—in spite of everything. So love yourself,
  and nourish the seeds within you.

Celebrate you.
Begin now. Start anew. Give yourself a new birth.
Today.
You are you, and that is all you need to be.
You are temporary. Here today and gone tomorrow.
But today. Today can be a new beginning, a new thing,
  a new life.

YOU CANNOT DESERVE
THIS
NEW
LIFE

IT IS GIVEN
FREELY

THAT IS THE MIRACLE
CALLED GOD

SO CELEBRATE
THE MIRACLE
AND
CELEBRATE
YOU

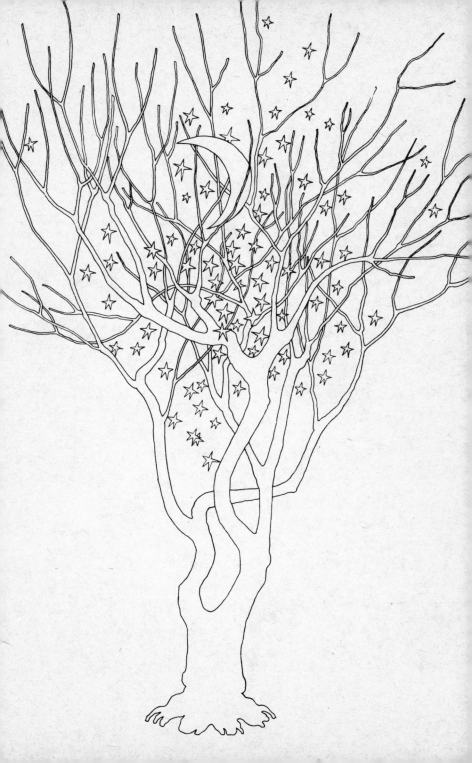

Reading Suggestions

There are just a few suggestions I would like to offer
for those who wish to read more in pursuit of the idea
of celebrating the temporary:

Bernard Gunther. *Sense Relaxation.* New York: Collier
Books, 1968. (A Book of Experiments in Being Alive.)
Paperback. $2.95.

Bernard Gunther. *What to Do Till the Messiah Comes.*
New York: Collier Books, 1971. Paperback. $4.95.

Edwin M. McMahon and Peter A. Campbell. *Please
Touch.* New York: Sheed and Ward, 1969.
Paperback. $2.95.

Alan W. Watts. *The Wisdom of Insecurity.* New York:
Vintage Books, 1951. Paperback. $1.65.

79 10 9 8 7